Tiny Island Stories

Tiny Bird

Published in the United Kingdom by:

Tiny Island Press
1 Bromley Lane
Chislehurst
Kent BR7 6LH, U.K

Copyright © Iris Josiah, 2012
Illustrations by Jane-Ann Cameron
Design & layout by Re-shape Invent

A CIP record of this book is available from the British Library
Printed 1 November 2012

ISBN: 978-0-9572728-4-2
Printed in the United Kingdom

Tiny Bird was a chirpy little bird. He had a tuneful little voice and flew all over Tiny Island.

Tiny Bird loved to fly and would FLY and FLY and FLY. He would fly from east to west and north to south of Tiny Island. And sometimes, he would fly to the neighbouring Blue Island and Yellow Island.

On Blue Island, the sky glowed bright blue and on Yellow Island, the sun shone bright yellow. Blue Island was home to some of the most beautifully coloured and cheerful birds.

So peaceful was Blue Island that Tiny Bird would FLY and FLY and FLY for days and days without meeting anyone.

But Tiny Bird had a secret which he had not told anyone on Tiny Island.

Tiny Bird loved to sing and
would SING and SING and SING.
At night, he sang to the moon
and by day, he sang to the sun.
But Tiny Bird did not tell anyone.

Instead, when he met Tiny Hen, Tiny Goat, Tiny Pig or any of the other animals on Tiny Island, he would simply say, 'good-day,' and off he went on his way.

'Well,' said Tiny Bird one day, 'I've kept my singing a secret for much too long.'

So he flew to the market where he could be seen by everyone.

'Good morning,' he said.

'Good morning, good morning,' they replied.

And he SANG and SANG and SANG.

Then He flew to the east. He flew to the west.

'Good morning,' he said to everyone.

'Good morning, good morning,' they replied.

And he sung the sweetest song.

He flew to the north. He flew to the south.

'Good morning,' he said.

'Good morning, good morning,' replied everyone.

And he SANG and SANG and SANG.

Then he flew to the towns and he SANG and SANG and SANG.

Then he flew to the villages.
And on his approach, he could
be heard by everyone.

'Good morning,' he said.

'Look, it's Tiny Bird,' cried Tiny
Hen. 'Oh, what sweet, sweet
voice you have.'

'Look, it's Tiny Bird,' cried Tiny Pig.

And Tiny Bird folded his tiny wings and landed.

'What a beautiful voice you have,' cried everyone.

'Thank you. Thank you,' said Tiny Bird.

And he SANG and SANG
and SANG to everyone.